For Clara —T.R.

randomhousekids.com

ISBN 978-0-7364-3643-4 (trade)
ISBN 978-0-7364-8227-1 (lib. bdg.)

Printed in the United States of America

10 9 8 7 6 5 4 3 2 1

The Kitchen Catastrophe

By Tennant Redbank

Illustrated by Alan Batson

Random House New York

Berry hopped up and down. Her long bunny ears quivered, and her pink bunny nose twitched. *Mmmm, mmm, mmm.* She could tell by smell alone that the peanut butter pet treats were almost done!

Berry had a sixth sense for baking. She knew when a batter needed more flour and when a soup needed more pepper. She could tell if dough needed to rise and when a sauce was about to boil. But Berry also had something even more important. She had her fantastic kitchen in the Pawlace!

Berry looked at her sturdy stone oven. She ran a loving paw along the edge of the white sink. She sighed. A good kitchen was the best baking tool of all.

She sniffed. The treats smelled done! She pulled on her oven mitts just as— *DING!*—the timer went off.

"They're ready!" Berry sang out. She peeked into the oven. Two trays of peanut butter pet treats sat inside. The edges were golden brown. Heart prints marked the tops. They were *paw*fect!

Berry bounced again. She couldn't help it. Then she made herself be still. She had to be careful not to mess up the treats. She reached in and took out the first baking tray.

"Aaaah-ooooooooh!" A happy howl echoed down the hall outside Berry's kitchen.

Berry smiled. That was Chauncey the corgi puppy. If Berry had a sixth sense for baking, Chauncey had a sixth sense for knowing when Berry's baking was ready.

All Berry's friends, from Petite the pony to Sultan the tiger, loved her treats. But Chauncey loved them the most.

Berry placed the first tray on the counter. She pulled the second tray from the oven.

"I smell yum, yum, yummy snacks!" Chauncey called. She tore around the corner and through the kitchen door. "I smell peanut— Oooh!"

Berry raised her head just in time to see Chauncey's paws slip on a wet spot on the floor. The little dog slid forward. She braced her paws, but they found nothing to grip. Chauncey slid across the floor . . . right into Berry!

The baking tray flew from Berry's paws, and treats scattered everywhere. The tray hit a box of baking powder above the cooktop. The box spilled into a pot of boiling water. The water foamed and overflowed onto the oven, the counter, and the floor.

"Watch out!" Berry yelled. She and Chauncey scooted out of the way just as a mixing bowl slid off the counter. The batter splattered the walls and stove.

There was a *POP!* as a blue spark shot up from the oven. It was followed by a fizzling sound.

Then—*drip, drip, drip.*

Water dripped from the oven to the floor.

"Oops," Chauncey said.

Berry put her paws over her eyes. Her beautiful oven! Her beautiful kitchen! They were a mess.

"Oh no!" Berry clenched her paws and stamped her foot. Then she saw that Chauncey was watching her with sad puppy-dog eyes. Chauncey probably felt awful!

"It's all right," Berry said. "We just have to clean up."

"Clean up," Chauncey repeated. "I can

do that!" She dashed off to get a mop.

"Are you okay?" a voice asked. "We heard a crash!"

Berry looked up. Her friends stood in the doorway. There was Petite the pony, Treasure the kitten, Pumpkin the puppy, and Sultan the tiger. Dreamy the kitten was there, too—and usually nothing woke her up from an afternoon nap.

Even Ms. Featherbon, Whisker Haven's cheerful hummingbird, had come to investigate.

Treasure looked around the kitchen. "Meowzers, Berry," she said. "What happened?"

"Well—" Berry began, but Chauncey jumped in.

"It was all my fault. I must have slipped," Chauncey said, waving the mop. Ms. Featherbon ducked as it swung past her head.

"I bumped into Berry," Chauncey went on, "and messed everything up!"

"Messes can be fixed," Ms. Featherbon said.

"Absolutely," Petite agreed. She placed her front hooves on a rag and pushed it across the floor. "We'll have the kitchen cleaned up in no time!"

The other pets grabbed brooms, brushes, buckets, and bubbles and set to work.

"Thanks!" Berry said. Then her smile faded. "I'm really worried about the oven." She turned a knob on the front. *Zzzzzzffffftt.* The oven didn't light. It just fizzled.

"Deary-dearest me," Ms. Featherbon said. "Who can we get to fix it?"

Chauncey wagged her tail. "Me!" she said. "I can do that! I'm very handy!"

That's right! Berry thought. She had heard that Chauncey could fix anything. When Ms. Featherbon's birdbath was clogged, Chauncy got it moving. When Sultan's slide was a little wobbly, Chauncey tightened it. Berry did a little bounce.

Ms. Featherbon nodded. "Let's all give Chauncey some room." She shooed the other pets from the kitchen. Then she lifted her hat and pulled out a roll of wide yellow tape. Printed over and over on the tape in big letters was KEEP OUT. She strung it across the doorway.

Berry bit her lip. Chauncey would do a great job fixing the oven. But what should *Berry* do in the meantime?

"It'll be done soon, right?" she called to Chauncey.

Chauncey laughed. "I haven't even started yet," she said. "Go on! Have fun!"

Berry *baked* for fun. How could she bake without a kitchen?

"Why don't you come to my library?" Petite suggested. "We can read."

What a great idea! Berry loved to read, but she was usually too busy cooking.

"Sure!" Berry agreed. She hopped after Petite.

At the library, Petite nosed the door

open. Two levels of books filled the walls. Pillows were scattered around. A trough of apples for snacking stood in one corner.

Apples. *Mmmm.* If only Berry had a little cinnamon and some nutmeg, she could bake . . .

Oh.

For a moment, she'd forgotten about her oven. Her poor oven! Berry shook her head. She had to stop thinking about baking!

Petite trotted to the far end of the library. She pulled book after book from the shelf. Berry read some of the titles:

Alice's Adventures in Wonderland. Peter Rabbit. The Runaway Bunny.

"All the books in this section have bunnies in them," Petite explained.

While Petite pulled out more books, Berry fanned open the pages with her paw and began to read. Wow! It was true. White rabbits, brown bunnies, spotted hares, bunnies with floppy ears, and bunnies whose ears stood up straight. Bunnies filled the pages of these books. Bunnies just like her!

She looked at all the books in front of her. How many were there? She decided

to line them up to count. She stood them next to each other. One, two, three . . . ten, eleven, twelve . . . twenty-two, twenty-three . . .

Berry couldn't believe how many bunny books there were! Her ears quivered. Her nose twitched. She started bouncing on her back feet. *Bounce, bounce, bounce.*

"So many books!" Berry cheered. "So many bunnies! Hooray!"

She flung her arms wide. One paw knocked into the very last bunny book— *The Tale of Benjamin Bunny*—and *clunk!* The book fell over. It knocked into the book next to it, and *clunk!*—that book toppled, too.

Clunk, clunk, clunk, clunk.

One after the other, all the books fell, like dominos.

Berry covered her eyes with her paws. Oh, no! Another mess!

Then Berry heard a noise—a happy neigh and the stamping of hooves.

"Berry, that was genius!" Petite said. "Book dominos!"

Berry peeked out from between her paws. *Genius?*

She started to bounce up and down. "Can we do it again?" she asked.

Berry and Petite spent an hour lining up books and knocking them down. They lined up horse books. They lined up dog books. They lined up cat books and tiger books. Sometimes Petite read a few pages out loud. Sometimes Berry did, too.

Then they set up more books. With a flick of her hoof, Petite knocked over the first in a row. On the other end, Berry pushed down the last book. The books toppled toward each other and stopped— right in the middle. The last two held each other up!

Berry clapped her paws. "I love books!"

she said. "Can I borrow some to read? And . . . Oooh!" Berry bounced higher and higher. "I just had the best idea! I can make a book cake. I'll frost each layer to look like a different book!"

Berry's ears swiveled toward the door. Maybe her oven was fixed!

"Petite, I need to check on my oven!" she called over her shoulder as she hopped away.

Berry tore down the hallway. She ignored the KEEP OUT tape and pushed open the kitchen doors. "Is it done?" she called.

Chauncey sat in front of the oven. Around her was a heap of tools. "Not yet!" the corgi said. "But it's getting there." She loosened an oven part and dropped it to the floor.

Berry's ears drooped. "Oh," she said. "Thanks, Chauncey." She'd been so sure the kitchen would be ready! She slunk out into the hall. She leaned her back against the wall and slid down to the floor.

"Hey, Berry!" Treasure padded past with a pillow balanced on her head. "Is your kitchen ready?"

"Not yet," Berry said with a sigh.

"Why don't you come with me?" Treasure said. "Dreamy is having a slumber party!"

Berry tilted her head. A slumber party could be fun. "Okay!" she said. She hopped down the hall after Treasure.

Dreamy's bedroom was filled with pillows and pet beds of all types—fluffy, feather-stuffed ones. Lumpy, bumpy ones. Soft, fuzzy ones.

Dreamy opened one eye when Treasure and Berry entered. "You came!" she said happily. "Pick a spot."

Treasure settled down on a blue-and-white striped bed. Berry found a purple bed nearby. She plopped down in the middle of it and crossed her paws. "Now what?" she asked.

"Now we nap!" Dreamy said, closing her eyes.

Berry tried. She really did. But she just wasn't sleepy in the middle of the day!

"I thought a slumber party would be more exciting," she whispered to Treasure.

"Me too!" Treasure whispered back. "I thought we'd tell pirate stories or something!"

"Yeah!" Berry said. "Stories of a daring pirate bunny—"

"And a pirate kitten!" Treasure cut in.

"—who sail the seas armed only with their . . ." Berry paused. Treasure leaned forward.

"PILLOWS!" Berry finished, bonking Treasure over the head with a pillow. She giggled at the look of shock that crossed Treasure's face. Then the kitten broke into a grin. She reared back and flung her pillow at Berry.

Berry ducked. The pillow soared over her head, and . . .

. . . thumped right into the sleeping Dreamy!

Treasure gasped. Berry put her paws over her mouth.

Dreamy's eyes shot open. She blinked once. Then, quick as a flash, the pink kitten grabbed a pillow in each front paw.

"PILLOW FIGHT!" Dreamy cried.

Dreamy was a ninja pillow kitten. She spun. She ducked. She twirled and leaped.

Berry and Treasure were brave pillow-fighters, but they were both outmatched. Dreamy had spent most of her waking—and sleeping—life around pillows. She knew them inside and out.

"I give up!" Berry gasped, collapsing in giggles.

"Me too!" Treasure said.

Dreamy dropped her pillows. She curled up next to Berry and Treasure and purred.

"That was lovely, and so much fun," she said. "Every good slumber party has a pillow fight."

A feather landed on Berry's nose. She blew it away. Who knew pillows could be such fun?

"Pillows!" she said suddenly. "That's a great idea for a new treat. Cheddar pillow billows!"

"Mmmm," Dreamy said. "Sounds yummy."

"Maybe my kitchen is ready!" Berry bounced to her feet. "I'll go check!"

Berry hopped down the hall to the kitchen. She ducked under the tape. Chauncey was still sitting on the floor. Tools were still piled around her. And now—oh, woe!—the oven rack was on the floor, too!

"Almost done?" Berry asked. She nibbled nervously on one paw.

"Getting there!" Chauncey said. "But you still have time. Go! Have more fun."

More fun?

The books were amazing. And the pillow fight had been a blast. But what was Berry going to do now? She just wanted to bake!

"Why don't you go to Pumpkin's primp salon?" Chauncey suggested. "You need to relax."

The primp salon? Well, okay. Berry wasn't much of a primper. But a spa day could be nice!

Out in the hall, Berry passed Petite's library. She passed Dreamy's bedroom. She reached the primp zone and poked her head inside.

"Pumpkin, can I come in?" Berry asked. "Chauncey thinks I need to relax!"

Pumpkin was arched up over a floor mat. She raised her head.

"Sure!" she said. "Sultan and I were just stretching!"

"Hi, Berry," Sultan said, extending

himself from nose to tail on his own mat.

Pumpkin grabbed Berry's paw and led her over to a cushy chair. "Sit here," she said. "I know just the thing for you!" She brought Berry a fruity whipped drink.

Berry sipped it through a straw.

"Oooh," Berry said. "Are those raspberries I taste?" She really loved raspberries. They were especially good in homemade raspberry granola. Or raspberry chip bars. Or . . .

Berry shut her eyes.

"No!" she said firmly. "I'm not going to think about raspberries. Or baking!"

When she opened her eyes, Sultan was lying on his shoulders. His rear paws were stuck straight up in the air. He winked at Berry.

"Shoulder stand," he explained.

"What else can we do here today?" Pumpkin asked. She rested her chin on one paw. "I know! I could dye your cottontail purple!"

"I don't know," Berry said. Purple? Cottontails were supposed to look like cotton!

"Or I could put an orange streak on each of your ears!" Pumpkin continued.

"They would look like racing stripes," Sultan added. He had pushed back and stretched his paws long in front of him.

"Um . . . ," Berry said. She didn't need racing stripes!

"Or I can give you a fluff-out," Pumpkin said, tipping Berry's head to one side.

A fluff-out didn't sound so bad. Not like a purple tail or bunny-ear racing stripes!

"Okay," Berry said. "Let's go ahead with the fluff-out."

Pumpkin twirled happily. She led Berry over to the sink and washed her fur. The warm water felt nice, like when Berry did the dishes after . . .

She shook her head. No! She was relaxing. She wasn't going to think about her kitchen!

Berry settled down into a comfy chair. Pumpkin moved a hair dryer over Berry's head. Warm air blew softly on Berry's fur.

After ten minutes, Pumpkin turned the dryer off.

"I think you're done," she said.

Berry nodded. She couldn't remember the last time she had felt so relaxed.

Chauncey had been right to send her here!

Pumpkin lifted the hair dryer. "Oooh," she said. "Oooh. Um, well, look at that. Hmmm. Berry, are you part Angora rabbit?"

Angora rabbit? Wait, weren't they the really fluffy . . . ? Berry's eyes flew open after Pumpkin spun the chair around to face the mirror.

Aaaaaaaahhhhhhh!

Berry's fur stuck out in every direction. Her head looked like a big, furry dandelion puff!

Berry put both paws over her mouth.

Sultan came over to the chair. "Well," he said, "I can see why they call it a fluff-out."

A giggle escaped from behind Berry's paws. "A fluff-out!" she said. Berry,

Sultan, and Pumpkin looked at each other and burst out laughing.

Pumpkin grabbed a brush and a spray bottle of water. "Don't worry," she said. "I can fix it!" She started to brush Berry's fur down.

"Hmmm," Berry said thoughtfully. "A fluff-out, a fluff-out. You know, I could

make fluff-out biscuits. They would be big and puffy, just like my fur!"

When Pumpkin was finished, Berry hopped off the chair. "Thanks for the idea, Pumpkin!" she said. "And the relaxing! But I have to go check on my kitchen.

Berry hopped down the hall as fast as her bunny feet could carry her. She skidded around the corner and broke right through the KEEP OUT tape.

"Oops," she said, holding up a length of tape. She bounced over to Chauncey. The corgi was inside the oven with only her back legs sticking out.

"Is it done, Chauncey?" Berry asked, leaning in. Her words echoed in the open space.

Chauncey slid out of the oven. She pulled a dirty cloth from her pocket and wiped her paws on it. "It's almost done!" she said. "But you still can go and—"

"Have fun?" Berry wailed. "I've had

lots of fun already. I've read books and knocked them down! I've tried sleeping. I've had a pillow fight and a fluff-out. And they *were* fun. But everything made me think of baking. And all I want to do now is . . . BAKE!"

Chauncey nodded slowly. "I have an idea," she said. "Wait here."

Chauncey tore off down the hallway.

Where is she going? Berry nibbled on her paw. She hadn't meant to raise her voice. She hoped Chauncey didn't think she was mean. She was just worried about her kitchen.

Chauncey came back a few minutes later with Petite, Treasure, Dreamy, Pumpkin, and Sultan. The corgi pulled another piece of cloth from her pocket and wrapped it over Berry's eyes like a blindfold. Berry hoped this cloth was cleaner than the other one!

The pets whispered to each other. Berry heard cabinet doors opening and closing and the clatter of pots and pans.

"What's going on?" Berry asked. "I can't see!"

Berry felt someone take her paw. Whiskers tickled her cheek. "Here. Hold on to my tail," Treasure said in her ear. "We're going on an *adventure.*"

Treasure led Berry out of the kitchen and down the hall. "Okay, now we're at the stairs. Take three steps down," he told her.

Berry carefully hopped down three steps. At the bottom, she felt soft grass under her paws. "We're outside!" she said.

"That's right," Petite agreed. "Just a little farther."

Holding Treasure's tail, Berry crossed the grass. At first the sun was shining on her face. Then she felt shade. She smelled pine. "Are we in Whisker Woods?" she asked.

"Good guess!" Sultan said.

Berry heard a birdcall. The air felt damper here.

"Just a little farther," Dreamy told her.

Treasure led her forward. "Are we going to read books in a tree house?" Berry asked. "Or have an outdoor slumber party? Or . . . maybe we're going to a hot spring to primp!"

Pumpkin laughed. "It's even better," she said in Berry's ear. "You'll see."

Berry felt Treasure untie the knot at

the back of the blindfold. The cloth fell away from her eyes.

Berry was in a clearing in the woods. At the center was a small campfire. Her friends stood around it, holding pans, baking trays, oven mitts, mixing bowls, and food—fruit and berries and spices and nuts.

"Berry," Pumpkin sang out, "you're going to bake!"

erry bit her lip. Her friends were kind. But how could she bake without her kitchen, her oven, her sink?

Everyone was watching her. Well, she had the recipes in her head. She had her sense of smell. Maybe with the campfire and a creek . . .

Mmm, she knew what she could make!

Bounce, bounce, bounce. Berry's ears

quivered, and her nose twitched. She grabbed a wooden spoon in one paw and a bowl in the other.

"Petite, can you pick the best apples from the bag? Five green apples and five red apples," she asked. "Pumpkin, please crush some graham crackers, and Treasure, grind some cinnamon."

Pumpkin and Petite nodded. Treasure

gave her a salute. "Aye, aye!" she said.

Berry whirled around. She took some butter from one of the bags. She put it in a pot and held it over the fire to melt.

"Here are the apples," Petite said. Berry diced them and added them to the pot. She dropped in the cinnamon and the graham crackers. She stirred it all together.

She tasted it. "Nuts," she said. "And maybe some raisins." Sultan handed her a cup of raisins. "No, not black raisins. The golden ones will work better!"

Berry stirred in the nuts and golden

raisins. She put on her oven mitts and cooked the mixture over the campfire.

She sniffed. It smelled just right. "It's done!" she called. She took the lid off the pot.

"Who wants some?" Berry asked.

"Me!" the palace pets cried together. Berry dished out Apple-Cinnamon Bunny Bake for everyone.

She held the bowl under her nose. It looked pretty. It smelled delicious. But how would it taste? Could she bake . . . without her kitchen?

Berry closed her eyes and took a bite.

Yum!

It tasted every bit as good as what she made in the kitchen. In fact, maybe it tasted even better. There was something special about eating outside in the woods.

"Oh, Berry," Treasure said. "This is delicious!"

"It's the best thing you've ever made!" Petite said.

Berry blushed. "That's just because you love apples."

Sultan shook his head. "No, she's right. It's—"

A howl cut off his words. Something

was coming through the woods. It was . . .

Chauncey! She skidded around a tree and dashed into the clearing. "I smell something yum, yum, yummy," she said. "What did you make?"

Berry handed Chauncey a bowl of Apple-Cinnamon Bunny Bake. Chauncey gobbled it right up. She even licked the bowl. When the last bit was gone, Chauncey raised her head. "Oh! I forgot," she said. "The reason I came into the woods was to tell you . . . your kitchen is ready!"

Berry's heart began to beat faster.

Hooray! Her kitchen was fixed! Then she looked around at all her friends.

"That's okay," she told Chauncey. "I have everything I need right here. Good food and good friends."

She pulled the wooden spoon through the Apple-Cinnamon Bunny Bake. "So . . . who wants more?"